The Allotment

Tamsin Peake

House of Sharky Press

Contents

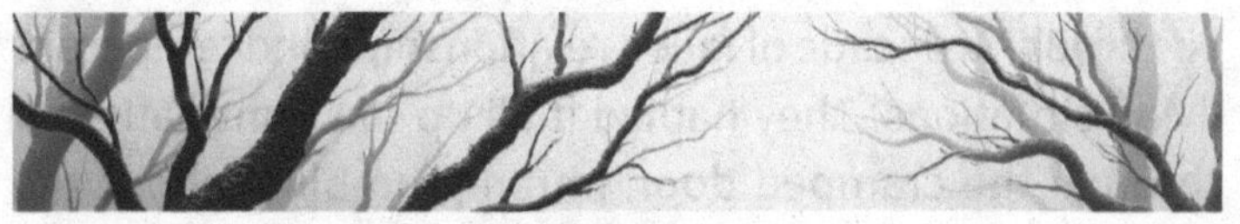

The Allotment

The letting agent had described the flat as "cozy with garden access," which Maya Kapoor discovered meant "small" and "you can see an overgrown patch of earth from the kitchen window." She signed the lease anyway because it was cheap, because Aylesbury was cheaper than High Wycombe which was cheaper than London, and because at thirty-four she was tired of house-sharing with people who left passive-aggressive notes about milk.

The flat was a ground-floor conversion at the back of a Victorian terrace on Alfred Street, all dark wood and narrow hallways, the kind of place that held onto cold even in summer. Maya's belongings arrived in her brother's van on a Saturday in mid March: a bed, a sofa, boxes of books she kept meaning to donate, kitchen things she'd accumulated through a decade of failed relationships and temporary living situations. They hauled it all up the front path and through the cramped door, Imran grumbling about the stairs even though there weren't any.

"You sure about this?" he asked, standing in the empty living room with his hands on his hips. "Aylesbury's a bit dead, isn't it?"

"That's the point," Maya said. "I need quiet. I need to actually finish the thesis."

He didn't argue. He knew about the breakdown, the medical leave from her PhD program, the six months she'd spent living on their sister's sofa in Slough, unable to look at her research notes without her chest tightening. The university had granted her an extension - one year to submit or forfeit. She had ten months left.

After he'd left, Maya unpacked in stages, stopping frequently to stare at the walls and wonder what she was doing. By evening she'd assembled the bed, arranged her desk under the window, and located the box containing her laptop and research materials. She made tea and toast and ate it standing in the kitchen, looking out at the patch of garden: a square of overgrown grass, a broken fence, and beyond it, what looked like allotments stretching away into the gathering dark.

Her phone buzzed. Her supervisor:

Hope the move went well. Let's schedule a check-in call for next week. No pressure, just want to see how you're settling in.

Maya typed back:

All good. Will send calendar availability tomorrow.

She didn't sleep well that first night. The flat made unfamiliar sounds - pipes knocking, floorboards settling, something that might have been mice in the walls. She lay awake listening to the silence underneath the noise, the particular quality of quiet that came from being in a place where you knew no one and no one knew you.

The first week passed in a haze of unpacking and avoidance. Maya set up her desk in the bedroom window where the light was best - or least worst, since the Victorian terrace blocked morning sun until nearly ten. She arranged her books on the cheap pine shelving from IKEA: research texts on agricultural history, theoretical works on labour movements, novels she'd been meaning to reread for years. She created a detailed work schedule in her planner, colour-coded by task type, with realistic daily word count goals and built-in buffer time for the bad days she knew would come.

By Tuesday, she'd already abandoned the schedule.

Wednesday she walked into town, needing to feel like she was accomplishing something. She registered at the GP surgery on Walton Street, filling out forms about medical history and current medications. The receptionist was efficient and impersonal. Maya added her name to the waiting list for a routine appointment, knowing she wouldn't call to book one unless something forced her to.

She found the nearest Tesco on High Street, bought basics: bread, cheese, eggs, tea, ready meals for the days when cooking felt impossible. She located the library, a modern building near the Waterside Theatre, all glass and open plan, the kind of space designed to feel welcoming. She got a library card, browsed the local history section out of professional habit, found nothing that interested her enough to borrow.

Aylesbury's centre was pleasant enough in a generic market town way. The Market Square with its Victorian clock tower and statue of John Hampden, whoever he was. Kingsbury Square with its shopping centre and chain coffee shops. Narrow medieval streets that suggested the old market town underneath the twentieth-century development: Cambridge Street, Temple Street, Church Street winding up toward St. Mary's. The usual mix of chain stores and local businesses struggling to compete.

Charity shops, estate agents, mobile phone shops, places selling vaping supplies.

She bought herself a coffee at a café in Kingsbury Square. A flat white, £3.20 was served in a cup that proclaimed the café's commitment to sustainability. Maya sat at a table by the window watching people pass. Thursday afternoon, not quite two o'clock. The café was half-empty. An elderly man read a newspaper in the corner. Two young mothers with pushchairs talked in low, tired voices. A teenager sat with a laptop and headphones, probably bunking off school.

Maya felt the particular isolation of being surrounded by strangers going about their lives. Everyone here had connections, histories, purposes. They knew where they were going and why. They had appointments to keep, people to meet, reasons to be out on a Thursday afternoon. She was just someone killing time, avoiding work, taking up space in a café because the alternative was sitting in her flat staring at her laptop and feeling the walls close in.

She finished her coffee and walked back slowly, taking the long route through the Bourbon Street housing estate where her flat was located. The estate had been built in the sixties or seventies, brick terraces and low-rise flats arranged around communal green spaces that were half-grass, half-concrete. Children's playground equipment, rusting and tagged with graffiti. An attempted community garden, mostly weeds. It wasn't grim exactly, just worn down, anonymous, the kind of place that accumulated people who couldn't afford anywhere else.

Thursday evening she heated up a ready meal. Chicken tikka masala, rice, naan bread, all in separate plastic containers, and ate it watching YouTube videos on her phone. Something about renovating old houses, people with money and time transforming Victorian wrecks into immaculate family homes. She watched three episodes before registering that she wasn't actually processing anything, just letting the images wash over her while her mind circled the same familiar grooves of anxiety and self-recrimination.

Friday morning she slept until eleven, having stayed up until three reading articles about nothing in particular. When she finally dragged herself out of bed, the flat felt oppressive. The heating was either off completely or on full blast - she couldn't figure out the thermostat. The kitchen window stuck halfway open, letting in cold air. The bathroom tap dripped no matter how tight she turned it.

She made tea and toast and sat at the kitchen table, forcing herself to open her laptop. Her thesis stared back at her: a Word document with 47,000 words of draft material, notes, half-formed arguments, sections that needed restructuring. The file was titled "Final_Thesis_Draft_v8" which was a lie. There had been at least twelve versions, probably more, but she'd stopped updating the number after a while.

Her thesis was on agricultural labour movements in early twentieth-century England, specifically the role of women in rural organizing. She'd spent two years researching it, working through archives in London, Oxford, Cambridge, tracking down collections of letters and meeting minutes and local newspaper reports. She'd accumulated thousands of words of notes, draft chapters that needed restructuring, a bibliography that ran to forty-three pages. It was good research.

Her supervisor had said so. "Solid work, Maya. Original argument. You're on track for a strong submission."

That had been eighteen months ago, before the breakdown.

Looking at it now felt like confronting evidence of a person she no longer was. Someone organized, capable, confident in her ideas. Someone who could read a primary source and extract meaning from it, who could construct an argument and support it with evidence, who could write 2,000 words in a day without feeling like they were pulling teeth.

She opened the most recent chapter - Chapter Four, "Women's Leadership in the Norfolk Agricultural Workers' Union, 1910-1914" - and read the first paragraph.

The participation of women in agricultural labour organizing during the early twentieth century has been systematically underestimated by historians focusing primarily on formal union structures and male leadership. However, examination of local records reveals that women played crucial coordinating roles, particularly in rural areas where traditional gender divisions of labour created spaces for female organizing outside formal institutional frameworks.

It was fine. Academic prose, properly referenced, making a clear argument. She'd written it six months ago. Reading it now, she felt nothing. No connection to the ideas, no sense that it mattered whether this argument was made or not.

She managed two hours before the familiar tightness started in her chest. The sensation of being observed, judged, found wanting. Her supervisor would read this and see through it, would recognize that Maya no longer believed in the work, that she was just going through motions, filling pages with words that meant nothing.

She closed the laptop and went outside, needing air, needing to be anywhere that wasn't inside her own head.

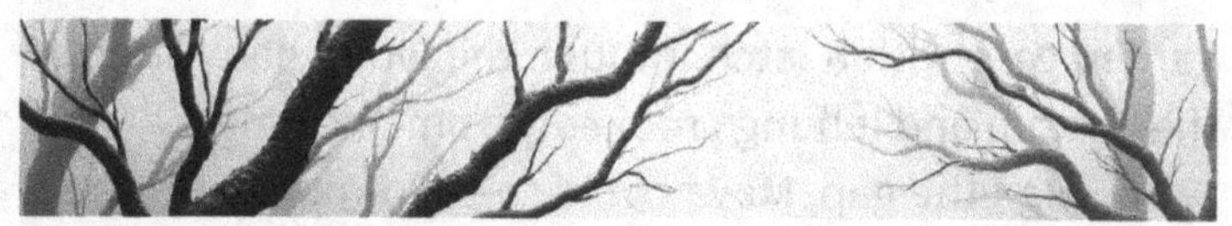

The garden was accessible through the kitchen door, which stuck in its frame and required a good shove to open. Maya stepped out onto cracked paving stones - York stone, maybe, grey and uneven, moss growing in the gaps - and looked around properly for the first time.

The space was perhaps ten meters by eight, enclosed on three sides by fence panels in various states of disrepair. The grass was shin-high, studded with dandelions gone to seed, their white heads bobbing in the slight breeze.

A buddleia had taken over one corner, its branches pushing against the fence. A washing line strung between two rusty poles sagged in the middle.

But it was the back fence that caught her attention. Or rather, what lay beyond it.

The fence was old, the wood grey and splintered, and at some point someone had installed a gate - a proper garden gate with a latch, though the wood had rotted at the bottom and it hung crookedly from one hinge.

Through the gap, Maya could see allotments: neat rectangular plots divided by narrow paths, some well-maintained with rows of vegetables emerging green from the dark earth, others overgrown and abandoned, reverting to nature.

She walked across the neglected lawn, her shoes getting wet from dew, and pushed the gate. It swung open with a creak that suggested no one had used it in months, maybe years.

The allotments stretched away in front of her. She estimated perhaps forty or fifty plots, all roughly the same size, arranged in a grid. Some had small sheds or greenhouses, others just open beds with wooden frames.

The paths between them were muddy but well-maintained, showing clear signs of regular use. Even on a weekday afternoon, mid-April, several people were working: an elderly man bending over a plot in the middle distance, someone else - she couldn't tell if they were male or female from this far away - digging at the far end, the rhythmic sound of spade striking earth carrying in the still air.

It was peaceful. Orderly. The kind of place where things grew according to predictable patterns, where effort yielded visible results, where you could measure progress in the height of seedlings and the weight of harvested vegetables.

Maya stood in the gateway for several minutes, just looking. She hadn't thought about gardening in years. Her parents had a small garden in the Slough house where she'd grown up, mostly lawn with a few shrubs, nothing ambitious.

Her grandmother, her mother's mother, had kept an allotment when Maya was very small, before arthritis made it impossible.

She had vague memories of visiting it: the smell of tomato plants, the taste of raspberries eaten straight from the cane, her grandmother's hands in the soil, explaining something about companion planting that Maya hadn't understood.

"Lovely, isn't it?"

Maya turned sharply, startled. A woman stood at the neighbouring fence - the fence between Maya's rented garden and the next property. She was elderly, perhaps seventy, wearing a waxed Barbour jacket that had seen better days and gardening gloves that were more patch than original material.

She had the kind of face that suggested decades of outdoor work - weathered, deeply lined, with sharp blue eyes that looked at Maya with friendly curiosity.

"Sorry," the woman continued, "didn't mean to make you jump. I'm Dorothy. Dorothy Linton. I live next door, number forty-three. You must be the new tenant at forty-five."

"Maya. Maya Kapoor. I moved in last week." She gestured toward the allotments. "I was just looking. I didn't realize they were back here."

"Been here since the seventies, these ones. Though there were allotments in this area long before that, even before Victorian times and these flats, I believe. Aylesbury's always been a market town, agricultural economy, lots of people keeping kitchen gardens."

Dorothy moved closer to the fence, clearly pleased to have someone to talk to. "Do you garden?"

"Not really. I mean, I like the idea of it, but I've never had the space. Always lived in flat-shares, student accommodation, that kind of thing."

"Well, you've got space now." Dorothy nodded toward the allotments. "Those plots back there - the allotment association runs them. Aylesbury New Town Allotment Association, though everyone just calls it the Association. There's a waiting list usually - quite popular, especially since that lockdown business, everyone suddenly wanted to grow vegetables - but I happen to know there's a plot coming available. Plot Seventeen. The previous tenant passed away in January, poor soul, and they've just finished clearing it out."

"Oh," Maya said, unsure how to respond to that. "I'm sorry to hear that."

"Don't be!" Dorothy smiled warmly. "She was ninety-three and lived a full life. Mrs. Oakes, her name was. Margaret Oakes. Had that plot for nearly forty years, tended it right up until the end. She's the one who told me about the vacancy, actually, before she died. Said she hoped the next person would look after it properly." Dorothy turned to face the allotments. "She was very particular about her plot. Treated it almost like a child."

Maya followed her gaze, trying to pick out which one might be Plot Seventeen. "I really don't know the first thing about growing vegetables. I'd probably kill everything."

"Well now. We all start somewhere. And the Association's very helpful - lots of experienced members willing to share knowledge. It's a good community. Very supportive. We meet every Sunday morning at ten, down at the main shed."

Dorothy paused. She turned to gaze at Maya, and something in her expression shifted - a kind of knowing sympathy that made Maya uncomfortable.

"Keeps you active. Gives you something to do with your hands. I find it helps when the mind gets too busy, you know? When you've got too many thoughts circling around with nowhere to go."

There was something uncomfortably perceptive in the way she said it, as though she could see Maya's unease, her floundering, the way she'd spent the last six months barely holding herself together. Maya felt simultaneously exposed and oddly comforted. At least Dorothy wasn't pretending not to notice.

"How much does it cost?" Maya asked, more to change the subject than because she was seriously considering it.

"Twenty pounds a month. Very reasonable, especially compared to what you'd pay for organic vegetables in the shops. And you get access to the tool shed, the composting area, all the communal resources. There's a water system - several butts connected to each other, rainwater collection. Very sustainable. Hugh - he's the chair of the Association - he's very keen on sustainable practices. Won't allow chemical fertilizers or pesticides. Everything has to be organic."

"That sounds... strict."

"It's for the best. Better for the soil, better for the environment, better for you when you're eating the food you've grown. Hugh knows what he's talking about. He's been gardening for forty years, longer probably. His family's been in Aylesbury for generations."

Dorothy adjusted her gardening gloves.

"If you're interested, come to the meeting on Sunday. I'll introduce you to Hugh. And if you decide you want Plot Seventeen, well, I'd be happy to show you the ropes. I'm in Plot Eighteen, right next door to it, so we'd be neighbours twice over."

She laughed at her own observation, and Maya found herself smiling back, only slightly registering the finger of unease stroking her spine.

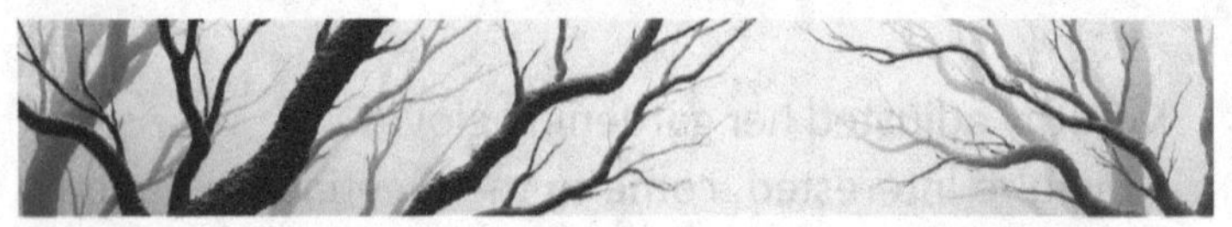

M aya hadn't intended to go. Sunday morning arrived grey and cold, threatening rain, and she woke with her usual sense of dread at the empty day ahead. She'd managed to work Saturday - four hours total, producing maybe 800 words that would probably need to be rewritten, but still, it was something. Progress. Evidence that she wasn't completely incapable.

But Sunday stretched ahead with nothing to fill it. She could work, but the idea of opening her laptop made her chest tighten. She could walk into town, but Aylesbury on a Sunday would be mostly closed, deserted, and the prospect of wandering aimlessly through empty streets felt more depressing than staying in the flat.

She could call her mother, but then she'd have to answer questions about how she was settling in, whether she was eating properly, making friends, getting out of the flat, and she didn't have the energy to reassure anyone that she was fine.

By nine-thirty she found herself standing in the kitchen, drinking tea, looking out at the allotments through the window. She could see people arriving: walking along the path from the main gate, carrying tools or pushing wheelbarrows, gathering near what must be the communal shed.

Dorothy appeared from her own garden, waved when she spotted Maya at the window, made a gesture that clearly meant *are you coming?*

Maya made a decision - or rather, she let the momentum of the morning carry her forward without thinking too hard about whether she actually wanted this. She changed into her oldest jeans and a jumper that wouldn't matter if it got dirty, put on her walking boots, and went out through the garden gate.

The allotments were laid out in a rough grid. She could see it more clearly now, walking along the main path. Perhaps forty plots in total, each roughly ten meters by five, separated by narrow paths of compressed earth and bark mulch. Some plots were immaculate: raised beds filled with what looked like early spring vegetables.

She recognized lettuce from the frilly leaves, maybe cabbage or something similar, definitely onions with their green spikes emerging from the soil. Neat paths of bark mulch between beds. Hand-painted signs indicating what was planted where: "Broad Beans - March 15th", "Potatoes

- Second Early - March 22nd", "Salad Leaves - Succession Planting".

Other plots were in various states of disarray: weeds reclaiming the earth, sheds listing sideways with moss-covered roofs, beds that had clearly been abandoned mid-season, bolted lettuces gone to seed, brambles creeping in from the edges.

Maya walked slowly, trying not to feel like an intruder, until she reached a larger shed structure at the centre of the complex. It was bigger than the individual plot sheds, perhaps four meters by six, with proper windows and a door, more like a small building than a shed.

A sign above the door read "ANTAA - Est. 1977" in faded paint.

A group of people stood outside, perhaps fifteen of them, holding mugs of tea and coffee and talking in low voices. They had the comfortable body language of people who knew each other well, who'd been gathering like this for years.

Maya suddenly felt very young and very foreign - not just ethnically, though she was the only brown -skinned person she could see, but foreign in the sense of being an outsider to a community with its own history and rhythms.

Dorothy saw her and waved, beckoning her over with enthusiasm. "Everyone, this is Maya! My new neighbour. She's interested in taking on Plot Seventeen."

The group turned to look at her - a collective assessment that felt friendly enough but unexpectedly thorough. Maya registered faces: an older couple, probably in their seventies, holding hands; a younger woman, maybe mid-thirties, with her hair in a practical braid; a man about Maya's age, thin and pale and slightly awkward; several other middle-aged and elderly people whose faces blurred together in her nervousness.

An older man stepped forward, extending his hand. He was perhaps sixty, with iron-grey hair cut short and practical, and the kind of solid, capable build that suggested a lifetime of manual work - broad shoulders, strong hands, the slight stoop of someone who'd spent decades bending over garden beds.

He wore corduroys and a waxed Barbour jacket, like Dorothy's but newer, well-maintained. His eyes were sharp and assessing.

"Hugh Tregarth," he said. His handshake was firm without being aggressive, his palm calloused.

"Chair of the Aylesbury New Town Allotment Association. We're pleased to meet you, Maya."

"Thank you. I hope I'm not intruding. Dorothy said I should come, but I don't want to waste anyone's time if - "

"Not a waste at all," Hugh interrupted, but gently. "Plot Seventeen's a good one. Excellent soil, good drainage, south-facing so you get plenty of sun. The previous tenant, Mrs. Oakes, kept it in excellent condition for nearly forty years. You'll be starting with a strong foundation, which makes all the difference for a beginner."

"I should tell you," Maya said quickly, needing to manage expectations, "I've never actually grown anything before. I don't know if I'll be any good at it. I don't want to take a plot if someone more experienced would do a better job."

This got a few chuckles from the group, and the younger woman - the one with the braid - smiled at'her.

"That's how we all started," she said, stepping forward. "None of us were born knowing how to grow vegetables. I'm Sian Hughes, by the way. I've got Plot Nine, just down from where you'd be. I'm happy to help if you need anything. Show you what to plant, when to plant it, how to avoid the common mistakes."

"We've all made those mistakes," added a stout middle-aged woman with a cheerful face. "I killed three batches of tomatoes my first year before I figured out I was overwatering them. I'm Penny Armitage, Plot Twenty-Four."

Others introduced themselves in a rush that Maya struggled to keep track of: Brian and Moira Dennison, the elderly couple holding hands, who'd been gardening together for forty years and had Plot Thirty-Two; James Whitmore, the pale shy man in his twenties, who mumbled something about Plot Six and working nights; Marcus Stone, a weathered man in his fifties who gave Maya a long, assessing look before nodding once and saying nothing; Helen and Thomas something-or-other, a couple in their forties with matching fleece jackets; Peter and Caroline and Diane and Richard, names and faces that blurred together in Maya's nervousness.

"We meet here every Sunday at ten," Hugh explained, gesturing to the group gathered around. "General maintenance, planning, sharing resources. It's informal but regular. And we have work parties once a month - the last Saturday - where everyone pitches in on communal tasks. Clearing paths, maintaining the fences, managing the composting bays, that sort of thing."

"The expectation," he continued, his tone becoming slightly more formal, "is that you keep your plot reasonably tidy and productive. We're not strict about it - we understand people have different amounts of time and energy - but we do expect commitment. This isn't just about growing vegetables, you see. It's about community. About being part of something. About maintaining this space for everyone's benefit."

There was an intensity in the way he said it that made Maya pause. It was just gardening, wasn't it? Growing vegetables in allotted spaces. But Hugh spoke as though it meant something more, something deeper.

"Mrs. Oakes understood that," Hugh added. "She was one of our core members - been here since 1983, when she first moved to Aylesbury. Forty years of dedication to her plot, to this community. She'll be missed, but we're grateful to have the opportunity to pass her work on to someone new."

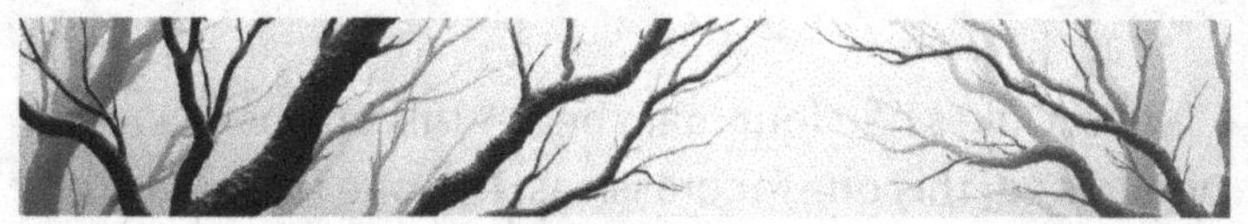

D orothy was already leading Maya away from the group, toward Plot Seventeen. The others returned to their conversations, though Maya felt their attention following her - curious, assessing, waiting to see if she'd fit in.

The plot was indeed in good condition. Better than good, actually. The beds had been recently cleared, their wooden frames solid and level, the earth inside dark and rich-looking, recently turned. The paths between beds were neat, lined with bark mulch that was relatively fresh, not yet decomposed into the soil.

A small wooden shed stood at one corner: perhaps two meters by two meters, painted dark green, the paint old but maintained, with a proper door and a padlock hanging open on its latch.

Dorothy walked Maya through the layout, pointing out features.

"Mrs. Oakes had four main beds—this one here was her potato bed, this one for brassicas, this one for salad crops and quick-growing things, and this larger one at the back for beans and peas and squashes. Good rotation system. She was very particular about not growing the same family of vegetables in the same bed two years running—helps prevent soil diseases."

Maya nodded, trying to absorb information she didn't fully understand. She knew vaguely that crop rotation was important but had no idea how to actually implement it.

"The shed's got everything you need," Dorothy continued. "Her daughter—lives in Australia, came back for the funeral and to sort out the estate—said to leave it all for the next tenant. Tools, seeds, pots, everything. Mrs. Oakes was very organized. You'll find it's all labelled and sorted."

"That was generous of her. The daughter, I mean."

"I think she felt it was what her mother would have wanted. Mrs. Oakes loved this plot. Spent most days here, especially after her husband died. I think this place kept her alive longer than she'd have managed otherwise." Dorothy touched one of the bed frames, her expression distant. "She was ninety-three when she passed. That's a good life. A full life. But still, you miss people."

"How did she die?" Maya asked, then immediately worried the question was insensitive. "Sorry, I don't mean to pry—"

"No, it's fine. Old age, really. Natural causes. They found her in her flat—she lived on Mandeville Road, nice little place she'd been in for thirty years—peaceful in bed. Her daughter said it looked like she'd just gone to sleep and not woken up. Best way to go, really."

Dorothy's expression shifted, became slightly troubled. "Though I do sometimes wonder if the plot missed her, you know? If plants can sense these things. I swear the beds looked sad after she was gone, like they were waiting for her to come back."

Maya didn't quite know how to respond to that. It was the kind of thing people said sometimes—anthropomorphizing plants, attributing feelings to gardens—but there was something in Dorothy's tone that suggested she meant it more literally than metaphorically.

They stood in silence for a moment, looking at the neat beds, the carefully maintained paths, the small shed with its hanging padlock.

"Well," Dorothy said eventually, shaking off whatever mood had caught her, "shall we look inside? See what you're inheriting?"

The shed was packed but organized. Maya had to duck slightly to enter—the door frame was barely five and a half feet high, designed for an era when people were smaller or less concerned with comfort. Inside, weak sunlight filtered through a small window, illuminating accumulated equipment that spoke to decades of careful gardening.

The walls were lined with hooks holding tools: spades and forks and hoes in various sizes, all clean, the metal parts oiled to prevent rust. Hand tools hung from a pegboard: trowels and dibbers and pruning shears and secateurs, each in its designated spot, outlined in marker pen so you'd know where to return them.

On shelves were clay pots in various sizes, stacked neatly; bags of compost and different types of fertilizer, all organic by their labels; balls of garden twine; packets of plant labels; seed trays; and dozens of glass jars containing saved seeds, each jar labelled in careful handwriting.

"Runner Beans - Painted Lady - 2023" "French Beans - Blue Lake - 2023"

"Tomatoes - Money-maker - saved August 2023""Lettuce - Lollo Rosso - 2022"

"Peas - Kelvedon Wonder - 2023"

There were at least fifty jars, maybe more, arranged by type on two shelves that ran the length of the back wall. Maya picked one up—the runner beans—and looked at the seeds inside. Dark red and black, kidney-shaped, perfectly dry. Professional quality, carefully saved.

"Mrs. Oakes was very serious about seed saving," Dorothy said, watching from the doorway. "She said it was important to maintain genetic diversity, to keep old varieties alive, to not depend on seed companies. Hugh taught her, years ago. He's very keen on heritage varieties, traditional methods."

On a small shelf near the window were notebooks—four of them, spiral-bound, their covers worn soft with handling. Gardening journals, Maya realized, pulling one down. Mrs. Oakes had recorded everything: planting dates, weather conditions, yields, observations about soil and pests and companion planting.

The most recent one started in January 2023, less than four months ago. Maya flipped through it, reading entries in the neat, slightly shaky handwriting of someone elderly but still careful:

March 15th: Planted first early potatoes - Charlotte variety. Bed 1 prepared with well-rotted manure from Hugh's compost. Good tilth. Weather mild but rain forecast.

April 3rd: Lettuce germinated in trays - Lollo Rosso, Tom Thumb, Little Gem. Will transplant when true leaves appear. Noted aphids on Plot 14 - mentioned to Marcus, who says he'll deal with it organically.

The entries continued through the summer, detailed and meticulous. August: harvests of beans and tomatoes and courgettes, notes about which varieties did well and which struggled. September: clearing summer crops, planting winter vegetables, preparing beds for spring. October: the last harvests of squash and pumpkins, putting the plot to bed for winter.

The final entry was from December 28th, just three weeks before Mrs. Oakes died:

Last harvest of kale from Bed 3. Still producing well despite frost. Bed rotation plan for 2024: potatoes in Bed 2, brassicas in Bed 4, legumes in Bed 1, mixed salads and alliums in Bed 3. Need to add lime to Bed 3 in early spring - pH getting too low for the brassicas I want there next year. Plot holding well through winter. Soil structure good. Another year nearly done. I find myself grateful for this place, for the routine of it, for the way it anchors me to the turning of seasons. Hugh says we're custodians, not owners, and I believe that's true. We tend the land for those who'll come after us.

Maya read the entry twice, feeling something catch in her throat. There was something poignant about reading the garden plans of someone who wouldn't live to see them implemented, the careful preparation for a spring that came too late.

"She knew," Dorothy said quietly from the doorway. "Not that she was about to die—she wasn't ill, it really was sudden—but she knew that the plot would outlive her.

They all do, if you tend them properly. The plot will still be here long after we're gone, producing food, being tended by whoever comes next."

Maya set the notebook back carefully on its shelf. The shed smelled of earth and wood and something else—dried herbs, maybe, or the particular scent of saved seeds, organic and slightly musty. It felt lived-in, loved, the accumulated space of someone who'd spent decades caring about this work.

"I'll take it," Maya said suddenly, surprising herself. "Plot Seventeen. I'll take it."

Dorothy's face lit up. "Oh, that's wonderful! Mrs. Oakes would be so pleased. Come on, let's go tell Hugh. He'll get you sorted with the paperwork."

The paperwork was simple. Hugh had the lease agreement with him—a single sheet, photocopied and filled in by hand. Maya read through it: twenty pounds per month, minimum one-year commitment, agreement to abide by the association rules, maintain the plot in good order, attend monthly work parties. She signed it and handed over forty pounds—two months up front, as requested.

"We'll get you a key for the tool shed," Hugh said. "And you're welcome to anything in Mrs. Oakes' shed—her daughter said to leave it all for the next tenant. There's tools, seeds, plant labels. Everything you need."

The group welcomed her with the kind of practical warmth that comes from shared purpose. They showed her the communal areas: the tool shed, well-stocked with spades and forks and hoes; the composting bays, steaming slightly in the cold air; the water butts for irrigation; the notice board covered with gardening tips and local information.

"We'll get you started with some easy crops," Sian said. "Potatoes are good for beginners—hard to kill. And salad leaves, maybe some beans. Nothing too ambitious for the first season."

Maya spent the rest of the morning at Plot Seventeen, exploring Mrs. Oakes' shed. It was packed with accumulated equipment: clay pots in various sizes, bags of compost, hand tools arranged neatly on wall hooks, jars of saved seeds labelled in careful handwriting.

She flipped through one of Mrs. Oakes's gardening journals again, glancing through the meticulous record of planting dates, weather conditions, yields, observations about soil and pests.

Maya set the notebook back carefully and felt a strange sense of responsibility. She was taking over not just a plot of land but a project, a history.

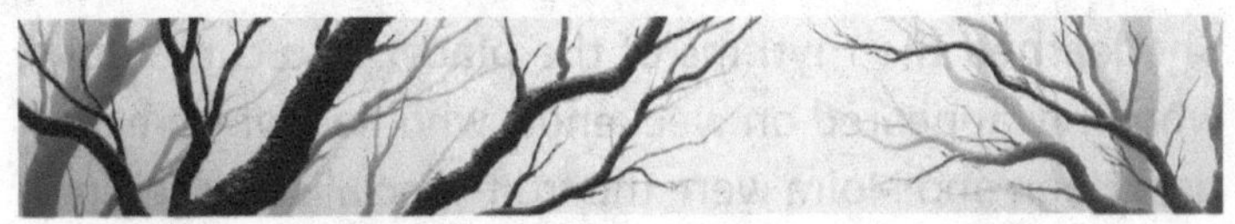

Over the following weeks, Maya fell into a routine. Mornings were for thesis work—she managed two or three hours most days before the anxiety became too much. Afternoons were for the allotment. She threw herself into it with the single intensity of someone who needed a distraction, reading books on organic gardening, watching YouTube videos on soil preparation, asking endless questions of Sian and Dorothy and anyone else who'd listen.

She planted early potatoes, following Sian's instructions. She sowed lettuce seeds and rocket and radishes. She dug over the beds, removing weeds and stones, adding compost from the communal bays. Her hands developed blisters that hardened into calluses. Her shoulders ached. She slept better than she had in months.

The allotment community absorbed her gradually. Sunday meetings became the anchor point of her week.

She learned the rhythms of the place: who came daily, who only appeared on weekends, who had which expertise. Brian and Moira were the fruit specialists—their plot was lined with raspberry canes and currant bushes. James grew vegetables with obsessive precision, his rows perfectly straight, everything labelled and timed. Marcus kept mainly to himself but would occasionally offer terse advice that turned out to be valuable.

Hugh was omnipresent, moving between plots, offering guidance, organizing work parties. He had an easy authority that people responded to. Maya watched the way others deferred to him, seeking his approval for their planting plans, asking permission to make changes to their plots.

"He's been chair for twenty years," Dorothy told her one afternoon. They were working side by side, Dorothy in her own plot, Maya in hers. "His family's been in Aylesbury for generations. He knows everything about local growing conditions, soil types, weather patterns. We're lucky to have him."

There was something in Dorothy's tone—not quite reverence, but close. Maya had noticed it in others too: a particular quality of respect that seemed to go beyond ordinary appreciation for a knowledgeable volunteer.

"What did he do before he retired?" Maya asked.

"He was a teacher. Geography and history at the Grammar School. Very well respected. He's written a book about Aylesbury's agricultural history—self-published, you can get it at the bookshop in town if you're interested. It's very good. Very thorough."

Maya made a mental note to look for it. She was curious about Hugh, about the intensity she sometimes caught in his manner when he talked about the allotments, about tradition and connection to the land.

By late April, her first crops were ready. The radishes came up crisp and peppery, their skins bright pink. The lettuce grew in loose, frilly heads, darker green than anything she'd bought from the supermarket. Maya picked a handful one afternoon—the outer leaves of several plants, as Dorothy had taught her, leaving the centres to keep growing—and carried them back to her flat in a canvas bag.

She made herself a salad that evening: lettuce, radishes sliced thin, a simple dressing of olive oil and lemon. The first bite was a revelation. The lettuce tasted alive in a way she hadn't known vegetables could taste—dense, sweet, complex. The radishes had a clean heat that cleared her sinuses. She ate the entire bowl, then went back to the plot and picked more.

Over the next week, she ate her harvest daily. Salad leaves for lunch, radishes as snacks, the first tender shoots of the broad beans Sian had shown her how to eat raw. She felt better than she had in months. Clearer. Stronger. The constant hum of anxiety that had been her companion for so long seemed to quiet. She woke before her alarm, eager to get to the plot, to put her hands in the earth, to tend the beds that were producing this perfect food.

"You're glowing," her supervisor said during their weekly video call in early May. "Aylesbury must be agreeing with you."

"I've been gardening," Maya explained. "Growing vegetables. It's... centring."

"Whatever it is, keep doing it. Your last chapter draft was excellent. Really sharp thinking. You're clearly in a good headspace."

Maya ended the call and looked at her hands. The calluses had thickened, her palms developing a layer of toughness she associated with manual labourers. Her nails, which had always been brittle and prone to breaking, had grown strong and fast. She'd had to trim them twice in the past week. And her hair—when she ran her fingers through it, it felt thicker, coarser, as though each strand had been fed from within.

She attributed it to the outdoor work, to eating well, to having purpose and routine. This was what health felt like. What connection to something real felt like.

The early potatoes came ready in mid-May. Hugh showed her how to check them, sliding his fingers into the soil at the base of the plant, feeling for the tubers.

"Wait until the flowers have finished," he said. "Then you know they're ready. You can fossick around for early ones without disturbing the whole plant – but check by hand first—don't dig blind or you'll damage them."

Maya harvested a few handfuls that evening: small, golden-skinned potatoes, each one perfect. She boiled them simply, dressed them with butter and salt, ate them with the reverence they deserved. They tasted like earth, like sunlight stored in dense, waxy flesh. She ate until her stomach hurt, unable to stop.

That night, she had her first dream about the plot. She was standing in Plot Seventeen at dusk, her hands buried in the soil of the centre bed, and she could feel something beneath her fingers—not roots, not stones, something else, something that pulsed with slow rhythm, something that recognized her. She woke with dirt under her nails even though she'd showered before bed, black crescents that took serious scrubbing to remove.

The first work party happened on a Saturday in late May. Maya arrived to find the entire allotment community gathered: perhaps thirty people, more than she'd realized were members. Hugh organized them into teams with military efficiency.

One group was assigned to repair fencing along the perimeter. Another was to clear and repair the communal paths. A third—including Maya—was tasked with preparing a new communal bed for growing vegetables that would be donated to the local food bank.

They worked for three hours, stopping halfway for tea and biscuits that Moira had brought. The atmosphere was convivial—people joking, sharing gossip, swapping tips. But there was also something else, an undercurrent of seriousness. When Hugh called everyone together at the end to inspect the work, they gathered in near-silence, waiting for his assessment.

"Good work," he said finally. "Very good work. The beds look excellent. The paths are clear. The fence will last another season." He paused, looking around the group. "I'm grateful to all of you. For your commitment. For your understanding of the continuity."

That phrase again: The Continuity. As though the allotments were more than just shared vegetable plots.

After the work party, as people were putting away tools, Maya found herself talking to James. He was a quiet presence at the allotments, arriving early and leaving late, speaking little but always absorbed in his work.

"How long have you been doing this?" Maya asked.

"Four years. Since I moved to Aylesbury." He straightened up from coiling a hose. "It helps. The routine of it. Something about putting your hands in the earth."

"I know what you mean. I've been finding it... grounding."

James side-eyed Maya at the pun, Maya grinned back. He nodded. "Hugh says that's what gardening is—centring yourself in the real, in the cycle of growth and decay. He says we've forgotten how to be grounded, most of us. We drift. The allotment teaches us to stay in place."

It was the most Maya had heard James say at once. There was something almost liturgical in the way he spoke, quoting Hugh like scripture.

"Do you come to all the meetings?" she asked.

"Every Sunday. And I try to make the evening sessions when I can."

"Evening sessions?"

"On Fridays. Hugh does workshops—advanced growing techniques, companion planting, soil management. They're optional but really useful if you want to develop your practice."

"I didn't know about those."

"He usually invites people once they've been here a few months. Once they've demonstrated commitment." James smiled slightly. "You will be invited, I'm sure. You're clearly serious about this."

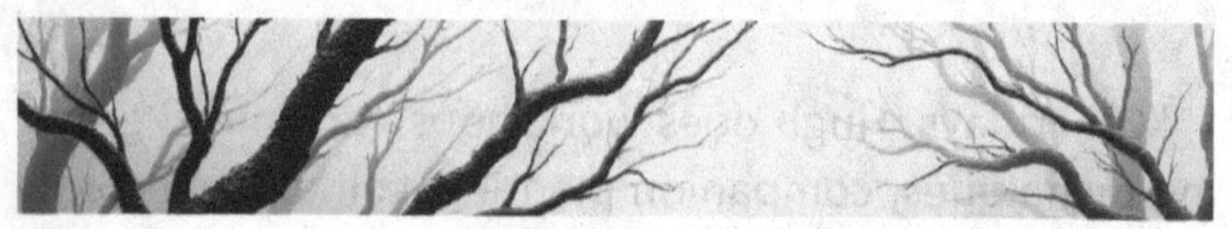

T he invitation came the following week. Maya found a handwritten note tucked into the door of her shed:

Maya—I've noticed your dedication to Plot 17. If you're interested in deepening your practice, we hold informal workshops on Friday evenings at 7pm. This week we'll be discussing heritage varieties and the importance of seed saving. You'd be very welcome. —Hugh

Maya wasn't sure why the note made her slightly uneasy. Perhaps it was the phrase "deepening your practice," with its suggestion of something more than amateur gardening. Or perhaps it was just the formality of the handwritten note when everyone else communicated by text.

Still, she was curious. And she was making progress on the thesis—she'd drafted two chapters in as many weeks, more than she'd managed in the previous six months. The allotment was working as Dorothy had suggested it might:

giving her hands something to do, her mind something to focus on that wasn't her own inadequacy.

Friday evening arrived cold and clear. Maya walked to the allotments at quarter to seven, her breath visible in the air. The place looked different in the dusk—the neat plots taking on strange shadows, the sheds becoming dark shapes against the darkening sky.

Light showed from the main shed. Maya knocked and entered.

Inside, eight or nine people sat on folding chairs arranged in a rough circle. Hugh stood at the centre, beside a table covered with small envelopes and what looked like old books. The others—Sian, Marcus, Dorothy, James, and a few Maya didn't know well—looked up as she entered.

"Maya," Hugh said, warmly. "Come in. We were just about to begin."

She took a seat next to Dorothy, who smiled at her. The shed smelled of earth and creosote and something else—herbs, perhaps, or dried flowers.

"Tonight we're talking about heritage varieties," Hugh began. "About the importance of maintaining genetic diversity, of keeping alive the crops that grew in this soil centuries before the modern seed companies homogenized everything."

He picked up one of the envelopes. "These are runner bean seeds—Painted Lady variety, been grown in Buckinghamshire since at least the seventeenth century. And these"—another envelope—"are Aylesbury Prizewinning carrots, a strain developed locally in the 1880s and nearly lost until a few of us began saving seeds fifteen years ago."

He talked for perhaps twenty minutes about the importance of seed saving, about genetic diversity, about maintaining local adaptations. It was all sensible, scientific, the kind of thing Maya might have heard at any gardening club. But there was something in Hugh's tone, in the way the others listened with such focused attention, that felt different.

"Our ancestors understood something we've forgotten," Hugh said. "That the relationship between land and people is reciprocal. We don't just take from the soil. We give back. We tend it, we feed it, we maintain it. And in return, it sustains us. Not just physically, but spiritually. The land holds memory. It holds continuity."

"When we grow heritage varieties, when we use the same beds that were used a hundred years ago, we're not just gardening. We're participating in something older and deeper."

He paused, looking around the circle. "That's what this place is really about. That's what Mrs. Oakes understood, what all the long-term members understand. The allotments aren't just for growing vegetables. They're for maintaining connection. For rooting ourselves in place, in history, in the land itself."

Maya found herself nodding along, caught up in the rhetoric. It made sense. It felt true, or at least meaningful.

"We have a particular responsibility here," Hugh continued. "This land has been cultivated continuously for at least three hundred years. It's documented in the parish records—this area was part of the common fields before enclosure, and even after enclosure, it remained in productive use."

"Think about that. Three hundred years of people putting their hands in this soil, growing food, saving seeds, passing knowledge down. We're the current link in that chain. We have a duty to maintain it."

After the formal talk, Hugh distributed the heritage seeds—small envelopes for each person, carefully labelled. "Plant them according to the instructions," he said. "Save seeds from the best plants. Next year, we'll trade among ourselves, maintaining the genetics, keeping the lines strong."

As people prepared to leave, Hugh touched Maya's arm. "Could I have a word?"

The others filed out, leaving them alone in the shed. Hugh closed the door.

"I wanted to say," he began, "that I'm impressed with how you've taken to this. You're a natural. You have the right temperament—thoughtful, methodical, respectful of the process."

"Thank you," Maya said, surprised by how grateful she felt hearing this.

"I wonder if you'd be interested in taking on a bit more responsibility. Plot Seventeen is one of our foundation plots—one of the oldest, with the best soil. Mrs. Oakes treated it as something of a trust. She understood that some plots are more important than others, not in terms of productivity, but in terms of... continuity."

"I'm not sure I understand."

Hugh smiled. "The allotment isn't uniform. Some areas have been cultivated longer, more intensively. Some have better connection to the underlying geology, to the water table. Plot Seventeen is special in that regard. Mrs. Oakes knew it. She treated that plot not just as her garden but as a kind of anchor point. Does that make sense?"

Not really, Maya thought, but she nodded.

"What I'm asking," Hugh continued, "is whether you'd be willing to maintain that tradition. To think of your plot not just as your space, but as something you're stewarding on behalf of everyone. The association. The history. The land itself."

"What would that involve?"

"Nothing onerous. Just commitment. Regular tending. And occasionally, when asked, allowing your plot to be used for communal purposes—experimental beds, heritage variety trials, that sort of thing. In return, you'd have support from the more experienced members, access to our more restricted seed banks, guidance on developing your practice."

It sounded reasonable. Vaguely cultish, perhaps, but in the harmless way that any group with its own jargon and traditions might seem to outsiders.

"Sure," Maya said. "I'm happy to do that."

Hugh's smile broadened. "Excellent. I had a sense about you. That you'd understand."

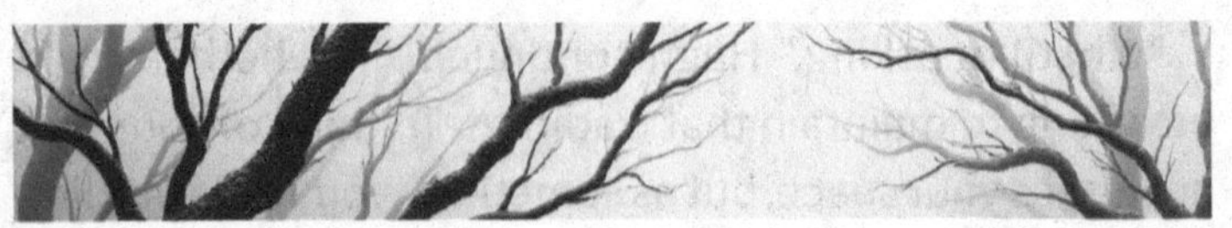

O ver the next month, Maya's involvement with the allotments deepened. She attended the Friday workshops regularly—they covered everything from companion planting to lunar gardening to the historical uses of various herbs. She learned to save seeds, to make compost, to brew comfrey tea for fertilizer.

Her plot flourished. The lettuce and radishes kept producing. The potato plants grew strong and healthy. The broad beans climbed their supports, heavy with pods.

She ate from the plot daily now, sometimes exclusively. The vegetables from the supermarket tasted like cardboard in comparison—wan, lifeless, grown in sterile media and shipped hundreds of miles. Why would she eat that when she had this?

But she also began to notice things that made her uneasy.

The workshops had started including longer sections on what Hugh called "land wisdom"—folk traditions around planting, harvest rituals, the spiritual aspects of cultivation. Some of it was interesting in an anthropological way: the stories about Lammas loaves and corn dollies, about the ceremony of the last sheaf.

But some of it felt stranger, less grounded in folklore and more in something Hugh seemed to have developed himself.

"The land needs acknowledgment," he said at one workshop in late May. "It needs to be seen, to be recognized. Our ancestors understood this. They made offerings—the first fruits, the best of the harvest. Not because they were superstitious, but because they understood reciprocity."

"What kind of offerings?" Maya asked.

"Depends on the tradition. Grain, obviously. Sometimes flowers. Sometimes... other things." Hugh's expression was serious. "The point is the gesture. The recognition that we're not just taking, we're participating in a relationship."

After that workshop, Maya mentioned it to Sian, trying to gauge whether others found Hugh's rhetoric as intense as she was beginning to.

"He can be a bit much," Sian admitted. They were working side by side, Sian helping Maya plant out her bean seedlings.

"But he knows what he's talking about. And honestly, I think he just really cares. About the place, about maintaining it properly. Better too much enthusiasm than not enough."

"Have you ever done the offering thing? The reciprocity stuff?"

Sian paused, her hands in the soil. "Yeah. Some of us do a small thing at midsummer—add some enrichments to the topsoil, plant some flowers at the centre plot, that kind of thing. It's harmless. Hugh organizes it. It's nice, actually. Makes you feel connected to something."

Maya didn't push further, but the unease remained.

The unease crystallized into something more concrete on a Sunday morning in early June when Maya arrived at the allotments to find a police car parked on the access road, its presence jarring against the peaceful ordinariness of the place.

A small crowd had gathered near the perimeter fence—perhaps fifteen people, standing in clusters, talking in low voices. Maya joined them, her stomach tight with a premonition she couldn't quite name. She spotted a teenager she recognised from the local greasy spoon at the edge of the group and nodded a greeting.

"What happened?" she asked "It's Padraig, right?".

Padraig gave a quick smile, attention returning back past the fence."They found a body," they said, voice hushed, half-excited, half-horrified in the way people get when confronted with death at a distance. "In the woods, just beyond the fence there. A dog walker spotted it this morning, called it in."

The woods were a thin strip of overgrown land between the allotments and the housing development beyond—perhaps fifty meters wide, dense with brambles and elder and sycamore saplings.

Maya had walked past the edge dozens of times but never actually went in. They had that neglected quality of spaces that aren't quite public and aren't quite private, land that belongs to someone in theory but isn't maintained or used for anything.

"Who was it?" Maya asked, though she wasn't sure why it mattered.

"Don't know yet. Police aren't saying much. But from what I overheard—" Padraig leaned in conspiratorially, "—it's been there a while. Weeks at least. Maybe longer."

Through the fence, Maya could see police officers moving between the trees, marking areas with tape, taking photographs. An ambulance sat further down the access road, waiting but in no apparent hurry. Whatever they'd found, it wasn't anyone they could save.

Hugh arrived perhaps twenty minutes later, parking his car—a dark green estate, old but well-maintained—and walking straight to where the senior police officer stood conferring with colleagues. Maya watched them talk: Hugh calm and authoritative, the officer taking notes, both of them occasionally looking toward the woods.

The allotment members stood around in clusters, no one quite leaving but no one doing any gardening either. Waiting for information, for permission to return to normal, for someone to tell them what this meant.

By mid-afternoon, the news had spread through the community, passed from person to person, embellished slightly with each telling. The body was that of a man, forties or fifties, likely homeless or transient. Been dead since March at least, possibly longer—hard to tell given the state of decomposition and the cool spring weather.

The police were treating it as non-suspicious but were investigating. Exposure, they thought, or perhaps drug-related, or some underlying health condition. These things happened. Tragic but not surprising. Homeless people died rough all the time, in doorways and parks and forgotten corners of towns, and usually no one noticed until the smell became undeniable.

Maya should have found this reassuring—tragic, yes, but mundane, a function of poverty and social failure rather than anything sinister. But instead she found herself doing mathematics she didn't want to do.

Mrs. Oakes, dead in January.

The homeless man, dead since March.

And before that—when had Sian taken over Plot Nine? Maya tried to remember. Sian had been here when Maya arrived in March, had already been established, her plot productive. So she must have taken it over sometime in the previous year. And the previous tenant? Hugh had mentioned him once, casually, in passing—something about him moving away, leaving the plot, no forwarding address.

Three people. Three deaths or disappearances. In roughly twelve months.

It was probably nothing. Probably coincidence. Old people died—that was normal, expected. Homeless people died—that was tragic but not unusual. People moved away without leaving forwarding addresses all the time, especially if they were running from debts or relationships or responsibilities.

But Maya couldn't stop thinking about it.

That evening, she did something she'd been putting off: she went into town, to the small independent bookshop on Market Square that Dorothy had mentioned, and asked if they had Hugh's book.

"*Aylesbury and the Agricultural Tradition*," the clerk said, scanning her computer. "Yes, we've got one copy. Local history section."

She found it on a shelf near the back: a slim volume, maybe 150 pages, self-published with a plain cover showing a black-and-white photograph of fields. "*Aylesbury and the Agricultural Tradition: Maintaining Connection to the Land*" by Hugh Tregarth.

Maya bought it and carried it home, feeling like she was doing something illicit, something Hugh wouldn't approve of. Which was absurd—he'd want people to read his book, wouldn't he? That's why people wrote books.

She made tea and sat at her kitchen table and started reading.

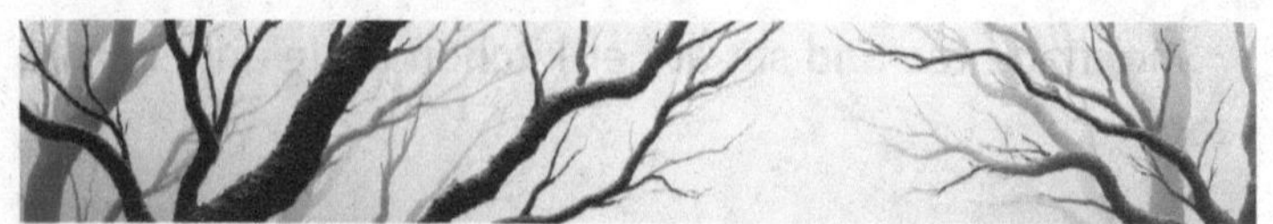

The first chapters were exactly what she'd expected: a competent, thoroughly researched history of agriculture in the Aylesbury area. The medieval open field system. The enclosure acts of the 18th and 19th centuries. The development of market gardening and decline of agricultural labour in the 20th century. Hugh wrote clearly and knew his sources, citing parish records, estate documents and surveys.

The academic in Maya recognised and responded to his craft.

But the tone shifted in the later chapters. Hugh started using language that felt less academic, more... devotional.

The relationship between people and land is not merely economic or practical. It is spiritual, rooted in deep time, in the accumulated wisdom of generations who understood that cultivation is not domination but partnership. The land requires acknowledgment, attention, and offering. In re-

turn, it provides not just sustenance but continuity, connection, meaning.

Modern agriculture has severed this relationship. Industrial farming treats soil as inert substrate, something to be exploited and discarded when its productivity declines. But the old ways understood that soil is alive, that it remembers, that it requires tending not just of its chemical composition but of its essential nature.

The allotment movement represents a return to this understanding. Those who tend small plots, who work the soil year after year, who save seeds and rotate crops and build up the tilth—they are maintaining the old compact, whether they articulate it in those terms or not.

There was a whole chapter on "folk practices"—the traditions Hugh had mentioned in the workshops. Planting by the moon. Leaving the last sheaf of grain in the field for the harvest spirits. Burying offerings at field boundaries to ensure good yields. Making corn dollies to house the spirit of the grain through winter.

Hugh wrote about these practices not as quaint historical curiosities but as genuine technologies, methods that worked even if the mechanism wasn't understood in modern scientific terms.

What might be viewed as superstition is understood here as acknowledgment. The land gives, and we must give in return. This is not metaphor. Our ancestors understood that certain places require certain attention, that some ground needs more than compost and crop rotation to remain productive.

They fed the soil not just nitrogen and phosphorus but something else - call it attention, call it acknowledgment, call it respect. The terminology matters less than the practice.

Maya read until the light faded and she had to turn on the kitchen lamp. She read until her tea grew cold and her back started to ache from sitting hunched over the book.

The final chapter was titled "Maintaining the Compact: The Aylesbury Allotments as Living Tradition."

Hugh described the history of the allotments, their establishment in 1977 on land that had been under cultivation for centuries before that. He talked about the founding members, about their commitment to organic methods, to heritage varieties, to maintaining connection to the land in an era of industrial agriculture.

And he talked about Plot Seventeen.

Plot Seventeen occupies a particularly significant position within the allotment complex. Historical maps show this area was the site of a medieval field boundary, likely used for communal grain cultivation as far back as the 13th century. The soil composition is distinct—deeper tilth, higher organic matter content, evidence of continuous cultivation over centuries.

The Ashburton family, who owned this land before the 1950s housing development, maintained it as productive garden ground even when surrounding fields were converted to pasture.

Tenants throughout the years have understood this history and treated the plot with appropriate respect. Their meticulous record-keeping and commitment to soil health over four decades created conditions for exceptional productivity.

But more than that, they understood—perhaps intuitively rather than intellectually—that certain ground requires more than ordinary tending. That the oldest cultivated places hold memory, hold expectation, and must be fed not just with compost but with acknowledgment.

Maya read the passage three times, trying to parse what Hugh was actually saying. *Fed with acknowledgment.* Memory. Expectation.

It could be metaphor. Probably was metaphor. A lyrical way of talking about soil health and the importance of respecting agricultural history.

But the language was so specific, so careful. And there was something in the way Hugh had spoken to her that first Friday workshop—*certain plots are more important than others*—that suggested he meant something more literal than she'd understood at the time.

She closed the book and sat in her kitchen for a long time, listening to the sounds of the evening. Traffic on the main road. Someone's television through the wall. The heating pipes knocking as they cooled.

And outside, beyond her garden fence, the allotments in darkness. Plot Seventeen waiting, its soil rich and black and deep, fed by decades of Mrs. Oakes' care and attention and something else Maya was only beginning to suspect.

She looked down at her hands. In the kitchen light, she could see the veins standing out more prominently than they used to—dark lines under her skin, branching like roots.

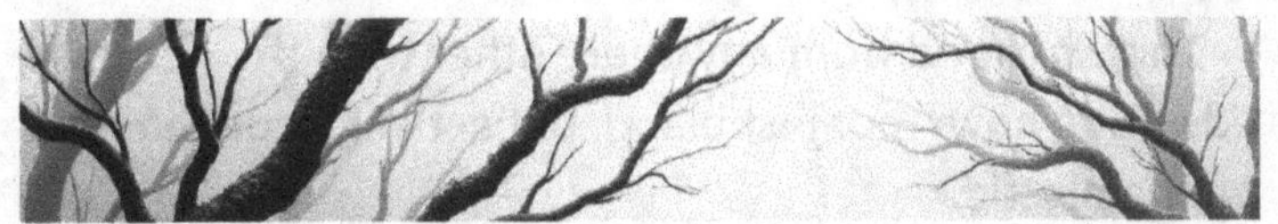

The summer solstice fell on a Friday. Hugh announced at the Sunday meeting that there would be a special celebration—a midsummer gathering at the allotments, starting at 9pm.

"Nothing elaborate," he said. "Just a chance to mark the turning of the year, to acknowledge the growth of the season. We'll light a fire, share some food, plant the traditional offering. Everyone's welcome."

Maya almost didn't go. The unease that had been building since she'd read Hugh's book had crystallized into something approaching dread. She'd started noticing other things, small things: the way her skin had taken on a slightly greyish cast, as though she'd been working outdoors too much, though the colour didn't fade when she stayed inside. The way her hair had thickened to the point where she'd had to buy a different brush, one with stiffer bristles.

The way food from anywhere other than the plot tasted wrong now—not just bland, but actively repellent, like eating plastic.

She'd tried to cut back on eating from Plot Seventeen, to see if it made a difference. She bought salad from Tesco, forced herself to eat it. Within an hour, she was bent over the toilet, retching. Her body rejected it completely.

So she'd gone back to eating from the plot. Because she had to eat something. And the vegetables from Plot Seventeen tasted right. Tasted necessary.

But she knew, in the part of her mind she was trying very hard to ignore, that something was wrong.

Dorothy caught her in the garden Thursday evening, asked if she was coming to the midsummer gathering.

"I don't know," Maya said. "I'm not feeling great. Might be coming down with something."

"Oh, you should definitely come if you're not well," Dorothy said, with the kind of misplaced enthusiasm that elderly people sometimes had about these things. "The fresh air will do you good. And Hugh always makes it special. You don't want to miss your first midsummer."

She said it as though it were inevitable that there would be more. As though Maya had already committed to years of midsummers, years of tending Plot Seventeen, years of being part of this community.

Maya found herself agreeing. Not because she wanted to go, but because the alternative—disappointing Dorothy, disappointing Hugh, failing to show commitment—felt impossible. The plot needed her. She couldn't explain how she knew that, but she did. Plot Seventeen needed regular tending. Needed her hands in its soil. Needed her attention and care and...

She stopped that line of thinking. She was just stressed. Reading too much into Hugh's dramatic language. Making connections that weren't there.

Friday evening arrived hot and close, the air heavy with the promise of storms that hadn't yet broken. Maya walked to the allotments at quarter to nine, wearing a long-sleeved shirt despite the heat because the veins in her arms had become more pronounced, worrying, a dark network that looked almost like mycorrhizal threads under her skin.

The gathering was already underway. Perhaps twenty-five people had assembled at the communal area, more than she'd seen at any single event. Someone had built a fire in a large metal brazier, the flames casting dancing shadows across faces. People stood around drinking wine and cider from plastic cups, talking in low voices.

Hugh spotted Maya and waved her over. He was dressed differently than usual—all in white, loose linen clothing that looked vaguely ceremonial. Others were similarly dressed, Maya realized. Sian wore a long white skirt. Marcus had on a collarless white shirt. Dorothy had wrapped her grey hair in a white scarf.

"I'm glad you came," Hugh said, handing her a cup of cider. "This is important. The first solstice you're here. A good time to establish your connection to the place properly."

Maya accepted the cup and sipped. The cider was strong, slightly bitter, with an herbal under-taste she couldn't identify.

As darkness fell complete—the long midsummer twilight finally giving way to full night—Hugh called everyone to gather around the fire.

"We're here," he began, "to acknowledge the turning point. The longest day, the moment when light begins to give way to dark, when the year shifts from growth to ripeness. Our ancestors marked this moment because they understood what it meant: that nothing lasts forever, that all things peak and decline, that we're bound to these cycles whether we acknowledge them or not."

He talked for perhaps ten minutes—about solar cycles, about agricultural traditions, about the importance of marking these transition points. Maya found it hard to concentrate. The heat from the fire was oppressive. Her skin felt tight. When she looked down at her hands, the veins were darker than they'd been that morning, almost black under the surface.

She drank more cider, hoping it would settle her nerves.

"The land gives to us," Hugh was saying. "All year, we take from it. We harvest its fruit. We eat what it produces. We are sustained by its generosity. And at midsummer, we give back. We acknowledge the debt. We maintain the balance."

He produced a woven basket from behind the table. "Each of you will take a portion of the offering. You plant it tonight in your plot, in the centre bed, at least six inches deep. We do this in honour of those who have held the compact before us." His voice slipped into an almost litanic cadence.

"We do this in honour of our place in this cycle. We do this and we keep the relationship alive."

People stepped forward, one by one, receiving something from Hugh's hands. Maya couldn't quite make out the words, faintly audible from each person, or see what he was distributing—something wrapped in cloth, small packages that each person took with solemnity before moving away toward their plots, torches bobbing in the darkness. Dorothy went forward. Sian. Marcus. James.

Then it was Maya's turn.

Hugh met her eyes as he placed the package in her hands. It was wrapped in rough cloth, tied with string. It felt dense, heavy for its size.

"Plant it tonight," Hugh said. "In Plot Seventeen, in the centre bed, deep. This is your contribution. Your acknowledgment of the relationship."

Maya took the package. Through the fabric she could feel shapes, irregular, organic. Her hands were shaking.

"Go on," Hugh said, and his voice was kind, gentle even. "It's just tradition. Just a gesture. But important."

Maya nodded and walked back toward Plot Seventeen. The cider had made her slightly dizzy. Or perhaps it was the heat, the smoke from the fire, the strange intimacy of the gathering in the dark.

At Plot Seventeen, she knelt in the centre bed. She set down her torch and with a hand fork began to dig. The earth was warm, still holding the heat of the day. Six inches, Hugh had said. She dug down, sifting soil through her fingers.

The soil here was darker than in the other beds. She'd noticed it before but hadn't thought much about it. Now, in the torchlight, it looked almost black. And there was something in it. Fragments of something white and porous. She touched one, brought her hand up to the light.

Bone. Old bone, crumbling into powder.

Her heart started to race. *Perlite?* No. She'd never needed to use it in her plot. *This was -*

She should open the package. She needed to know what she was being asked to plant.

But her hands wouldn't obey. They moved of their own accord, placing the wrapped bundle into the hole she'd dug, covering it with soil, patting it down. Her body completing the ritual while her mind screamed at her to stop, to look, to understand what she was doing.

Only when it was done—when the offering was planted and the soil smooth—did Maya manage to wrench back control. She stood up fast, stumbling slightly, her vision swimming.

Something was very wrong.

She looked down at her hands in the torchlight. The veins weren't just dark—they were moving. Pulsing. Branching. She could feel them extending, reaching, connecting to something beneath her feet.

Maya ran.

She didn't stop to collect her things from the shed. She didn't say goodbye to anyone. She just ran, bursting through the gate, sprinting along the access path toward the street.

Behind her, she heard Hugh calling her name, but she didn't stop.

At her flat, she slammed the door and locked it. Her hands were still shaking. She turned them over under the kitchen light, examining them.

The veins were dark, yes. But they weren't moving. She'd imagined that. The cider, the heat, the stress of the last few weeks—it had all combined to make her see things that weren't there.

She was having a breakdown. Again. Just like before. The pressure of the thesis, the isolation of Aylesbury, the intensity of Hugh's rhetoric—it had all been too much. She'd built up a paranoid fantasy about ritualistic murder and contaminated soil and...

Her phone buzzed. Dorothy:

> *Are you okay? Hugh is worried.*

> *Maya, It's Sian. Please let us know you're safe.*

Then Hugh:

> *Maya. We need to talk. What you saw tonight - you need context. This doesn't need to be difficult.*

Maya didn't reply. She went to her bedroom and pulled out her duffel bag. She'd leave first thing in the morning. Get on a train, go back to Slough, stay with her sister while she figured things out.

She paced the small kitchen, gathering chargers, her phone. The university would understand. She'd ask for another extension, explain that the accommodation hadn't worked out, that she needed—

A knock at the door made her freeze.

"Maya?" Hugh's voice through the wood, quiet, confidential.

"I know you're frightened. But we need to talk about this."

She said nothing. Hand flying to her mouth, she found herself drawing silently towards the door, unable to pull her attention from where his voice murmured, her other hand seeking the frame for support.

"You felt it, didn't you?" Hugh continued. "When you planted the offering. You felt the connection. That's good. That means the plot has accepted you. That means you're part of the continuity now."

Maya bit down on her hand to keep from making a sound.

"This is what Mrs. Oakes felt, at the beginning," Hugh said. "This is what we all felt. The recognition that the land is alive, that it chooses, that it needs certain things from us. It's frightening at first. But it passes. And what comes to you in return—the clarity, the purpose, oh! The belonging to something real and old and important!"

Silence. Maya could hear the scratch of his rough palm stroking the wooden door.

"It's worth it."

A pause.

"The offerings are necessary," Hugh said, and his voice had dropped lower, to a murmur, become almost reverential.

"The land must be fed. Not with violence - don't let your fear make this something nasty, Maya. It's not like that. The offerings are volunteers. People who are already dying, already lost. We give them purpose. We help them. We help them find meaning in their ending. Mrs. Oakes understood this. She contributed willingly, in the end. She became part of the earth she'd tended for forty years. She nourishes it still."

A tang of adrenalin on her tongue, she discovered she could move. She silently backed away into the bedroom.

"You've been eating from Plot Seventeen for weeks now," Hugh's voice rose, almost declamatory. "You've been nourished by soil that Mrs. Oakes fed. By soil that generations fed before her. You're part of the cycle now. Part of the continuity. You can't undo it, Maya. The roots are already in you. You felt them tonight. You know it's true."

She looked down at her hands again. In the darkness of the bedroom, with only the streetlight filtering through the curtains, the veins looked black as tar. And they were branching. She could see new tributaries appearing as she watched, fine dark lines spreading across her palms.

"I'm going to leave something on your doorstep," Hugh said. "Instructions. Information. History. When you've had time to process this, to understand it, you'll see that it's not what you feared. We're not monsters. We're gardeners. Stewards. We abide by the old ways. We keep the land alive. And in return, the land keeps us."

Footsteps walking away.

Maya waited, counting her breaths. When she was sure Hugh had gone, she crept to the front door and looked through the peephole. A package sat on the doorstep, wrapped in the same rough cloth as the offering she'd planted. Beyond it, the street was empty.

She didn't open the door. She texted her brother:

Need you to come get me first thing tomorrow morning. Early as possible. Will explain everything then.

He replied within minutes:

Shit, Sis. Everything ok?

No. But I'll be fine. Just come early. 6am if you can. Park on Bourbon Street.

A minute passed. The ellipsis flashed, disappeared, returned. Maya clutched her phone, nails digging into the palm of her other hand.

Wow. Sure. Ok. NP. Will be there.

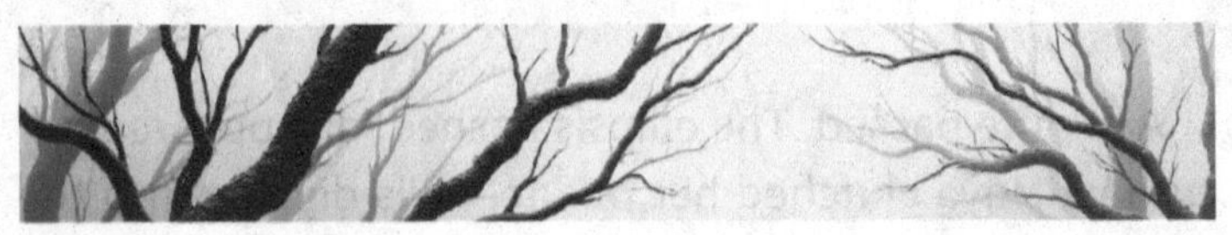

Maya didn't sleep that night. She sat in her kitchen, lights on, watching the allotments through the window. Torchlight moved between the plots for hours—people planting their offerings, completing the ritual, maintaining the compact with whatever waited beneath the soil.

At some point, she noticed she could hear something. Or not hear exactly—feel. A low vibration, a pulse, coming from the direction of the allotments. Unwelcome, the thought appeared. Plot Seventeen. Calling to her. Reminding her that she had responsibilities, that the plot needed tending, that she'd made a commitment.

She pressed her hands over her ears but it didn't help. The call wasn't audible. It was deeper than that. It resonated in her bones, in her blood, in the dark network of veins that was spreading through her body.

At 5:45am, she grabbed her bag and went out the front door, stepping over Hugh's package without looking at it. The street was grey with pre-dawn light. Maya walked quickly to where her brother would arrive, keeping her eyes forward, not looking back at the allotments.

Imran's van appeared at 6:02. She pulled open the passenger door before he'd fully stopped.

"Drive," she said, buckling herself in and pulling her hoodie over her head.

He pulled away. Maya watched through the mirror as her flat receded. No one followed. But she could still feel it—the pull from Plot Seventeen, the soil reaching for her, the roots that had already grown too deep to extract.

Imran turned towards her at the first set of traffic lights.

"What the hell, Miy, you look like shit," her brother said.

Maya looked at her hands. The veins were darker than ever, branching in patterns that looked less like human vasculature and more like mycelial networks, like the underground architecture of fungus connecting trees in a forest.

"Just drive," she said. "Please. Just - get me away from here."

Sucking his teeth, Imran put the van in gear as the lights changed. There'd be no details from his sister, he knew. Not until she was ready. Giving her knee a soft punch he settled in for a silent trip.

They drove south, through the awakening town, past the closed shops and empty market square. Out onto the A41. Maya kept waiting for the pull to fade, for the distance to break whatever connection had formed between her and the plot.

But it didn't fade. If anything, it grew stronger. By the time they reached Slough, Maya was gripping the door handle so hard her knuckles were white. Her skin had taken on a grey-green cast. Her stomach was cramping.

"I need to go back," she muttered.

"What?"

"Take me back. To Aylesbury. I need to go back."

"Maya, you just said you had to leave. You said—"

"I know what I said!" The words came out in wail. She felt like she was asleep. "I need to go back. I need to—I have responsibilities. The plot needs tending. I planted something and I need to check on it. I need to—"

She caught sight of Imran's aghast expression, stopped. Listening to herself. Hearing Hugh's words coming out of her mouth.

"Woah! No!" she said. "No, keep driving. Imran, take me to yours. I'm staying with you. I'm sorry. I'm not going back."

Her brother looked at her, worried. "Maybe we should go to A&E. You sound well weird, Miy."

"No - I'll be OK. Sorry - I'm fine. I just need some time away from there. I just need to sleep."

But she wasn't fine. Over the next three days, staying at her brother's flat, Maya got worse. The cramping in her stomach intensified. She couldn't eat anything—even water made her nauseous. The intermittent whine in her ears became relentless, making it difficult to notice when Imran spoke to her.

The veins continued to darken, to branch, spreading across her torso, down her legs, up her neck. In the mirror, she looked like a anatomical illustration, her circulatory system visible through skin that was becoming increasingly translucent.

When she asked Imran on that first day to look at her veins, he looked more anxious and suggested they go see his GP. She was careful to avoid mentioning them again after that, but still caught him looking at her with that crease between his eyes.

She dreamed of Aylesbury. Not images - but the place and her shape in it was embodied in sense dreams, of roaring winds, waking with her nostrils filled with complex dark aromas and a gnawing pang of longing in her gut. On the fourth day, she woke to find thin white filaments growing from under her fingernails. Not fungus—something else. Something that looked like roots.

She tried to pull them out. They hurt, rooted deep into the quick, and when she pulled hard enough to extract one, it came out trailing blood and something else, something pale and fibrous that looked like the mycelium she'd read about in Hugh's book.

She hid her bloodied tissues from Imran, kept her hands under the table.

Maya called Hugh.

"I need to come back," she said.

"I know," he replied. "We've been waiting for you."

"What's happening to me?"

"You're becoming sustenance. In a manner of speaking. The same way you've been feeding the plot here. It's reciprocal. You ate from Plot Seventeen. Now that you're not here to keep tending to its needs, it eats from you. That's the compact. That's the relationship."

"Make it stop."

"I can't. Neither can you. That's not how this is. But if you come back, if you tend the plot properly, if you keep up your end of the relationship—it will stabilize. You'll grow. You'll achieve homeostasis, balance. You'll become a true steward, like Mrs. Oakes was."

"And if I don't come back?"

Silence for a long moment.

"Then the plot will just take what it's owed," Hugh said finally. "One way or another. You can give it willingly—your time, your care, your attention. Or you can give it unwillingly. Mrs. Oakes chose the first option. She lived to ninety-three, tending her plot, in relationship with the land. Others have chosen differently. That's what you found in the woods. Someone who tried to run."

"Some people will simply never understand the true nature of sacrifice, Maya. But not you. I knew that when you were given to us. You are the right one for this calling. "

Maya ended the call.

She looked at her hands. The roots had grown longer overnight, thin white tendrils emerging from her fingertips, questing.

She had a choice, she realized. She couldn't stay here. Every day of trying to act close to normal, mask her horror at catching sight of the weirdness happening beneath the surface of her skin, knowing that all Imran saw was his sister apparently going mad again in front of him. It was horrible.

She could run further, could go to London, could try to disappear. But the plot would find her. It was already in her, had been since the first radish she'd eaten, the first lettuce, the first potato dug from soil that had been fed with decades of - offerings.

Or she could go back. Could tend Plot Seventeen. Could maintain the compact. Could live in relationship with something older and stranger than she'd ever imagined, something that fed her and fed on her in equal measure.

She thought about Mrs. Oakes. Ninety-three years old. Four decades tending the same plot. Dying peacefully in her sleep and then, presumably, being returned to the soil she'd cared for. Completing the cycle.

Was that so terrible? Was that worse than dying alone in a hospital, or in a nursing home, forgotten by every-one except the staff who changed the bedpans? At least Mrs. Oakes had died with purpose. Had died knowing she would continue, in some sense, in the soil of Plot Seven-teen.

Maya packed her bag. She booked a train from Slough, planning to leave when Imran would be on shift. She wrote him a letter, thanking him, reassuring him that she had an appointment with her regular doctor. She left, avoiding his worry and questions she had no idea how to answer.

I need to go back. I know. I'm so sorry. Thesis Freakout. I'm OK though. I'll be in touch soon. Love you Rahn.

She'd deal with his texts and calls later. Right now she knew what she must do.

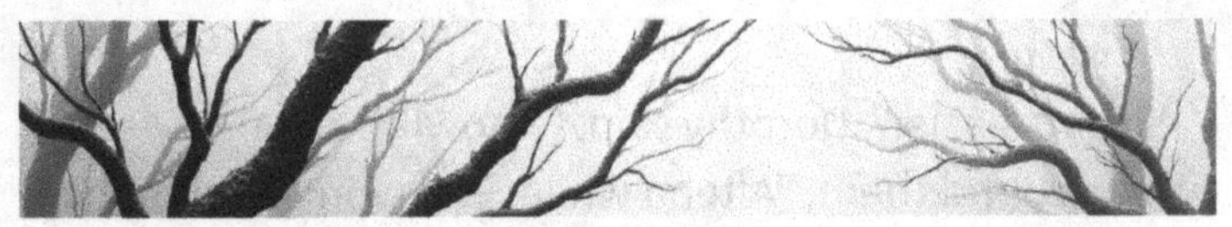

H ugh was waiting at the allotment gates. He smiled when he saw her.

"Welcome home," he said.

Maya walked past him, through the gate, along the path to Plot Seventeen. The soil called to her, welcomed her. She knelt in the centre bed and pressed her hands into the earth, and she felt the roots in her veins connect to something deeper, something vast, something that had been feeding and being fed for centuries.

The whine in her head stopped. The pain began to recede. The nausea evaporated. She could breathe again.

She stayed there, kneeling, her hands in the soil, for what felt like a very long time. Struggling to her knees, she looked around, Dorothy was there, watching from Plot Eighteen.

"It gets easier," Dorothy said. "Knowing all of -" She gestured around them. "After a while, you won't even notice. You'll just be part of it. Part of the continuity."

Maya looked down at her hands. The roots had stopped growing. The veins were still dark, but they were stabilising. Fed and feeding. Part of the cycle.

She went back to her flat that evening. The package at her front door had gone. She called her supervisor, said she'd been ill but was feeling better now, would have another chapter ready by next week.

The next morning she opened her laptop. Six messages from Imran, their sister Suki. She replied with the same calm, reassuring and - sane - tone she'd found for her supervisor.

She didn't even feel like she was pretending. Easier now, to reassure them, now that balance was returning. She hit send on the messages and slept for 12 hours.

The next few days moved like glycerine. She ate the produce some of the other plot holders delivered to her doorstep. She worked on her thesis. Soon after, she returned to her plot. If she dreamed, it was in silence, and she woke with the soft weight of Thanatos on her, calm, inert, and untroubled by the world.

She returned to the Sunday meetings and the Friday workshops. She harvested vegetables and ate them. She saved seeds. She kept up scheduled video meetings with her supervisor, her family. The crisis had passed and their concerns with it.

The weeks passed into months.

In August, she helped with the main harvest—potatoes and beans and tomatoes and squash. In September, she prepared the beds for winter crops. In October, she plant-ed garlic.

The dark veins in her hands became something she stopped noticing. The faint green tinge to her skin be-came normal. No one else around the town seemed to notice anything odd, and she suspected that she'd feel quite unconcerned even if they had. The way she could feel the plot's needs—more water, time to harvest, a bed that needed compost—became as natural as hunger or thirst.

They marked the Winter Solstice in December and shortly afterwards, she submitted her thesis. Dr. Maya Kapoor. She had a viva in February. She passed.

She got job offers. London. Oxford. Cambridge. All of them far from Aylesbury. She turned them down.

Instead, she took a part-time position at the local library. It didn't pay much, but it was enough. And it left her afternoons free for the plot.

By the spring, she'd taken on a second plot—Plot Eighteen, after Dorothy died peacefully in her sleep in March, at the age of seventy-six. She was returned to her soil, mixed with compost and organic matter, spread across the beds she'd tended for thirty years.

Maya scattered her ashes herself. It felt right. It felt like completing the cycle.

Hugh asked her to take on a leadership role in the association. She agreed. She had knowledge to share now. Experience. She understood the compact in ways that newcomers didn't, couldn't, not until they'd been here long enough. Not until they'd eaten from the soil. Not until they'd been tested, adventitious roots growing deep enough to anchor them.

A new tenant moved into the flat Maya had originally rented. A young man, anxious, working on something academic. She could see the stress in his posture, the way he moved like someone trying to outrun their own thoughts.

Maya knocked on his door one afternoon. Introduced herself. Told him about the allotments. His name was Ken.

"I don't know anything about gardening," he said.

"That's fine," Maya laughed. "I didn't know my broad beans from my brassicas when I moved here. We all start somewhere. And there's a plot that just came available. Plot Nine. Good soil. South-facing. The previous tenant moved away."

That was true. Sian had left Aylesbury last month, tried to relocate to Brighton, be near the sea. They'd found her three weeks later, in a car park, dead of what the coroner ruled as natural causes. Heart attack. Stress-induced. Common enough in people in their thirties, especially those with anxiety disorders, especially those who'd been under pressure.

She'd been returned to Plot Nine. Fed back into the soil she'd abandoned. The compact maintained.

Ken was looking at her with interest. "I've been thinking I need something. Some kind of routine. Something to do with my hands."

"I tell you, Ken, gardening saved me during my thesis. The plot would be perfect for you," Maya said. "Gives you something to focus on. Something real. You know?"

She smiled at him. A warm smile. A welcoming smile.

"Come to the Sunday meeting. I'll introduce you to Hugh. He'll get you sorted."

After all, the plots needed tending. The soil needed feeding. The continuity needed maintaining.

And there was always room for one more.

END

About the Author

Tamsin Peake is a member of the **House of Sharky** collective, writing short horror, speculative fiction, and crime with a focus on the uncanny and the ethically uncomfortable.

Their work often explores how ordinary spaces become unstable, and how patterns of care, silence, and belief shape what people are willing to endure.

Tamsin's short fiction is set across the UK and vicinity, with several stories rooted in Buckinghamshire. They publish new work regularly as part of an ongoing short horror series and works beyond.